I0537951

JANICE WILLOW...ASSASSIN

A Janice Willow Novel

By

Eddie J Martin

Assassin

Content

Janice Willow

Born: Detroit, Michigan

Age: 28

Race: Black

Height: 5'11

Weight: 143

Chest: 39, Waist: 23, Hips: 35

Schools: Downing Elementary, Rosa Park High School

Sports: Soccer, basketball, volleyball, karate, judo, mountain climbing

Employment:

1993-1994

Smell So Sweet Have - A- Dashers

1994-2005

United States Air Force

2005 to Present

Federal Government

Expertise: Assassin

CHAPTER 1

AGENT STONE WALKED into Commander Jenkins

office and was told to take a seat.

"Okay, let me have it, how bad is it?"

"Three agents are dead, two lost at sea, and one was last heard from in the Norwegian Alps. All of them went through Canon at one time or the other. We believe agent Sisley is in his lodge somewhere in the Swiss alps. Since she's a very attractive young lady, he may try keeping her there. What's it going to take to get to him?" Jenkins asked.

"Well, sir, we sent five of our best people and they got nowhere, the only thing I can think of doing is sending in Janice—Janice Willow! But, if we do that, we can be prepared to start a body count—she kills even when there's a chance to save."

"Well, this time, Agent Stone, we don't need a savior; we need an assassin to kill every one of those bastards who murdered our people. Has Janice been briefed yet?"

"Yes, sir, and all she asked was how many we wanted alive."

"What did you tell her, agent stone?"

"Zero! She was happy about that."

"What type of cover did you give her?"

"You'll love it chief, and so did she. Assassin!"

"Now, that is appropriate for her," he said. "An assassin killing a bunch of other assassins. Do a background check and make sure everything is set in place, and that her cover name is Miss Payne. How will she be dropped off at her location?" the chief asked.

"She'll go in on a commercial flight. There's no telling who will be watching."

"What about support aids and things like that?" Jenkins asked.

"She doesn't like that kind of stuff, chief. She has her pp2 with the silencer and that Japanese throwing knife. She never liked those other things since the time she kissed Simons with that poison in her teeth. She killed him in a matter of seconds even though it could have easily killed her. I think she'll rely on what she knows best—her few weapons, wits and body. But then, never say never."

Agent Stone and Commander Jenkins were an FBI special team. They had recruited Willow right out of the Air Force when they found out she was a serial killer and had been flying under the radar ever since she's been in the military—some say even before that. Since she was so good at what she does, they felt they should hire her. The other guys had theirs; why shouldn't they? They had no doubts that Willow was a killing machine, way before Jaws was created. She had the capacity to kill those she wasn't even instructed to kill. There's something in her that's just pure evil. So far, she's been doing a great job, but every now and then, they feared she could go rouge on them.

"HOW LONG will you be gone?" she asked.

"I have no idea, I'll call you." Willow had been living with a young lady of 25 for a few months to slow herself down—or so she thought. But after 6 months to a year, the killing spree came back to her. At least she knew how to get away from Keisha when those feelings started. She couldn't risk having her on her conscience, if she even had a conscience. She hadn't been on assignment for almost a year, and she was getting bored. Depending on what she encountered, she might be gone for a while. Keisha was an airline stewardess, so it wasn't like she'd be waiting around for her.

J. Canon Biography:

Italian, 42, single but with 3 kids by a previous marriage.

Business: transport / export in slave trade of young kids 6 through 12 years of age.

Mode of transport: helicopter, Learjet, 35 and 55ft, 75 and 111-foot yacht with a 12-man crew.

Homes in Rome, France, Australia, USA and Copenhagen.

Two other competitors were trying to move Canon out but he was determined to get to them first. Steger is in Australia, while Mr. Yen is in Korea. He was determined to hire the best assassin money could buy, hit the top, and the rest would fade away, or take them under his wing. It would make him larger by 50%. He decided to start with Mr. Yen in Korea since he was the smaller of the two. He gave Yen the opportunity to join him but he wouldn't take it. "Mr. Yen wants to play games with him. He'll be the first to go."

"Stager, he is the larger of the two and pretends to be the so-called kingpin of our trade. He'll learn better soon enough. The assassin that's coming in from Germany is supposed to be the best. She's being paid enough! My number one says they call her Ms. Payne; he should know he's hired a few for me but says she's the absolute best. We'll see how she does with Mr. Yen, and it wouldn't hurt to take out his number one so they would have no one to turn to."

"SISLEY, where you at, woman? Come in here, let me see how you look." Sisley Robinson, an agent, came into the den. She had been with the agency for three years. She was now given the assignment to take out Canon. She was wearing a sheer nightgown with only panties underneath and high heels. Sisley was white and tan by way of a tanning machine. She had brown hair cut into a bob, long neck and arms, and wide eyes with thick eyelashes. She had lips that could be used in magazine ads. She was 5 foot 8 and approximately one hundred and thirty-five pounds. Her breasts were the envy of most professional models, with nipples that were almost black, incased in a light brown circle. Her legs gave the impression she was standing on stilts and with high heels on. Plus, she smelled good.

"That's the way I like to see my girls. Now, go to the bedroom, I'll be there shortly."

"Ms. Payne, this is Carl."

"Yes," Willow said, a.k.a. Ms. Payne.

"We need you to proceed straight to Seoul Korea and take care of that job first. Is that a problem?"

"Not as long as the funds are deposited before I leave," she said.

"You can check your account; the funds will be there. Half now and half after the job is completed."

"Then, consider the job taken care of."

"And Miss Payne, there may be one or two with him. If you get the opportunity, they can go too."

"That'll be extra."

CHAPTER 2

The Hit

SEOUL, SOUTH KOREA. Willow stepped off Korean Southwest Airlines, flight 726. She strolled through customs, picked up her bags, and proceeded to the taxi stand. At the exit door, there were men holding up signs with people's names on them and one of them read: *Ms. Payne.* Willow hadn't been told there would be a ride waiting on her, so she stopped. "I'm Ms. Payne."

"Ms. Payne, I was told to pick you up by my dispatcher and take you to the Soong Sans Hotel."

"Just a minute," she said, and went to the side to make a call. "Did you send transportation for me at the airport?" she asked. The answer was in the affirmative. She went back to the driver and said, "Lead on!"

In her suite, Willow got undressed and took a bath in complementary bubble bath, put on lounge clothes, and poured herself a gin and tonic at the bar. She sat down and brought out the file on Mr. Yen. There was a 7 x 5 picture of him. He was an older gentleman, aged 62, and of Korean descent. He had gray hair that receded at the top. He was clean-shaven and had typical Asian eyes. He had a diamond earring in his left ear. He stood at 5 foot 2, and 145 pounds. Mr. Yen always wore Western-type clothes from the twenties—three-piece suits with a vest and suspenders, a pocket watch and chain, plus black and white high top boots.

Mr. Yen was a lover of the old gangster movies with actors like Humphrey Bogart, James Cagney and Peter Lori. When he wasn't in the bathhouse with three of his girls, he'd be watching an old-time gangster movie in his home theater. His number one man was Troy Lee, a gentleman of 42 years and a master of Kung Fu. Troy Lee takes care of the day-to-day workings of the organization and sometimes works as a bodyguard. Mr. Yen has one other man servant, who is with him on occasion when Troy Lee is absent. One of his homes is on the outskirts of Seoul, up on a small hill surrounded by an electrical bamboo fence with flowers intertwined within it.

Mr. Yen leaves his house three days a week to either see his mother in the nursing home on Mondays, to tend to his businesses on Wednesdays in the city—taking Troy Lee along with him, and to go to the market in town for fresh vegetables on Saturdays.

Willow felt she had enough information on Mr. Yen and the next day, she would scout the area around his home.

The next day, Willow rented a scooter and started touring the city. She eventually ended up on the road leading up to Yen's home. The road was 5 miles of two winding lanes with a steep cliff on one side, and larger hills on the other side. The road went past Yen's, but there was another leading a half mile into Yen's property.

Willow rolled by and saw what was in the file—bamboo fence and all. She rolled by the other end that went on for miles. After four or five miles, she turned around and headed back toward town and passed Yen's house.

After she passed by the second time, she had a good idea of how she was going to get to him and his number one. However, she would need the help of Agent Stone.

At 9:45 AM on Wednesday morning, Mr. Yen and Troy Lee were headed down the mountain for his usual weekly business meeting in his Rolls-Royce, which was armored and plated to protect him against small firearms. Mr. Yen and Troy Lee were discussing how to expand their business and to keep Canon at bay.

"The only solution I can see is to take our Mr. Canon out because he won't stop until he takes us out. He's greedy, there is enough business for us all."

"Look into it," Mr. Yen said to his number one. "Put it into operation if it seems feasible, as soon as you can. And Troy Lee..." At that moment, an explosion hit the automobile, as it was making its way downhill. The explosion knocked the automobile over the cliff and into the bottom of the canyon, then it exploded twice more.

Willow stood up from where she was kneeling on the slope above, put away the aircraft rocket launcher, and got on her scooter and headed back down the hill to town.

CHAPTER 3

Success

Carl walked into the den, where Canon was sitting in his lounge chair having a cognac and reading a book.

"Mr. Canon, look at this." He set his laptop down in front of him and opened it to a news program out of Korea.

Breaking news! Mr. Troy Yen, owner of Yen's Electronics, was killed today in a motor vehicle accident. While leaving his hilltop home, his auto failed to negate a turn and went over the cliff and burst into flames. In the vehicle was Mr. Yen, his driver, and his number on—Mr. Troy Lee. The accident is under investigation. It is believed that the vehicle was hit by some type of projectile. We will keep you informed.

"What you think about that? Didn't I tell you my girl was something else?"

"You surely did. When can I meet this lady?"

"Well, it's up to you, sir. As you know, she's under contract to knock off Steger in Australian. I guess I could pull her in before she takes care of him. I'll make the call."

"Do that, Carl. I'd seriously like to meet this lady. She intrigues me. To tell you the truth, I've never met a female assassin before. I'd like to do it now because we're going to be busy with this other business we'll acquire."

Willow was in the Philippines when she got the call that Mr. Canon wanted to see her. "But I'm almost at my destination. Can't it wait?" she asked.

"We appreciate your enthusiasm, Miss Payne, but when Mr. Canon calls... You know how it is."

"You're paying for it."

"Plus, we heard Steger is not in Australia now anyway; he left for Greece."

"When were you going to tell me that, Carl? After I got to Australia?"

"We just found out ourselves, Ms. Payne. Why don't you stop off in Manila for a few days before you come here, take a short holiday. By the way, you did an excellent job in Korea. Mr. Canon was very pleased.

"I'll see you in a few days then."

"JANICE is on line one," Agent Stone said to Agent Jenkins. "I'll put her on speaker phone."

"Agent stone?"

"I'm here, Janice. I have agent Jenkins here with me and we're both on speakerphone. Go ahead."

"I arrived in Manila at 3:45 local time. I was redirected by Conor's number one, Carl. He says Steger is no longer in Australia but in Greece. Nevertheless, Conor wants to see me. I don't know what about, but my next stop will be the Alps after a few days here. It was suggested; it wasn't my idea."

"That's great, Janice. Maybe you can locate our agent while you're up there. You have seen her file."

"Yes, sir. if she's there, I'll find her."

Korea, Jenkins said. great job!

"Yen wasn't a big loss and when I get to Steger, he won't be either. The big one is Canon but I can't touch him until I find the girl. He doesn't seem to be in such a rush for me to hit Steger once Yen was gone. For some reason, he wants to meet me."

"Curious, Janice. He's just curious about you."

"You know what they say about curiosity? It killed the cat."

"Find our agent, Janice," Jenkins said. "Find our agent!"

CHAPTER 4

Sisley

FOR THREE MONTHS, CANON has had me cooped up in this place. As nice as it is, it still feels like locked up to me. I should have knocked him off when I first got here but I can't sneeze without someone saying 'bless you', not to mention the cameras and listening devices. I was on my way to his room one night and it so happened that one of the other girls made up her mind to escape that same night and all hell broke loose.

They caught up to her and you could hear the screams for days. When she came back there wasn't a mark on her face, but her butt, back, and feet were something to behold. We must have worked on that girl for thirty days. After she got half-way right, they put her on one of Canon's cargo ships so she could service the crew. We never saw her again. The rest of them never thought about running after that. One of us for each day of the week, and Tuesday he rested, unless he went on one of his trips to see about his business holdings.

I've got to figure out a way to get to him, I thought. After being together would be the best time, but right after sex, he tells me to leave. I asked one of the other girls about that and she said, "It's because one girl tried to stab him when he went to sleep. She didn't fare too well after that."

"What will eventually happen to us once he gets tired of us?"

"We'll get moved out to a cargo ship to service the crew or to walk the streets. If we're still in pretty good shape, we'll wind up in a Geisha house in Japan. Our future doesn't look good. For now, just keep doing what you're doing and hope for the best."

Every now and then Carl will come in here trying to get a little bit, and a few of the girls have turned him on.

"Have you?"

"Sure, why not." He's a decent enough guy and Canon is not one of the best lovers I ever had.

"Does he know?"

"Oh, hell no, and no one's going to tell him. He would pitch a bitch and no one would be safe, including Carl."

"He won't be messing with you for a while because he knows you are his favorite, for right now anyway."

"All of us has been a favorite at one time or another. Now, I'm number two after you, then after you move out of favor, I'll be number three and you'll be number two, and on and on."

"What happens when you get to the end of the line?"

"Cargo ship," she said.

This is my first assignment for the agency and it looks like it may be my last. There is no opportunity to get to Canon unless something drastic happens. I can't even find a way to contact them. I'm sure they think I'm dead by now.

Back in Australia, Makin, Steger's number one man approached him and said,"Mr. Steger, have you heard about Mr. Yen in Korea? Never expected that."

"I did, that's no one but Canon. He's trying to take over everything. We can look for him to come after us next. Any idea who the hitter was?"

"Not yet, but we'll find out pretty quick. Give it time."

"What are you doing to protect our interests?" Steger asked.

"Well, sir. There is only so much we can do. Double the security at all our locations but I feel he'll be coming after us like he did with Yen."

"If you feel he's coming after us next, then we should get to him first. You may be right, Makin, you may be right."

CHAPTER 5

Mountainside

Ms. Payne exits from the helicopter at Canon's mountainside home where Carl is waiting for her.

"Welcome to mountainside. Did you have a nice trip?"

"I did, you still have snow up here, I see."

"The snow never goes away this far up the mountains, some stay all year round. I hope you bought a jacket. If not, I'm sure we can find you one. Mr. Canon is out skiing right now but he'll be back around lunch. Come, I'll take you to your room."

The room was more like a suite. There was a small bar, lounge chair, couch, and a king size bed, with hidden closets and clothes laid out on the bed in her size.

There was also a bath and sauna combo. The first thing Willow did was head for the bar and pour herself a gin and tonic. Then, she drew herself a bath and afterwards, took a nap on the bed. Less than thirty to forty-five minutes later, her phone rang in the room and Carl asked if she had rested. He said Mr. Canon would like to see her in the billiard room. A girl would come to escort her there as he didn't want her to get lost.

"That'll be fine. I'll be ready." The girl at the door looked more like a doll than a person. At 5 foot one and 98 pounds, she literally looked like a small doll. She was Japanese or Chinese, and when Willow opened the door, she had to look down and almost had to get on her knees to look her in the eye. Willow thought she was a little kid at first, until she looked closer.

"My name is Kim," she said, looking up at Willow. "I'm here to take you to Mr. Canon in the billiard room."

"Well, Kim, lead on."

Upon entering the billiard room, Willow saw a thirty-foot bar and chairs, a standard size pool table, pictures on the wall of Fast Eddie and other billiard superstars. Canon was just about to make his shot when Willow and Kim walked in. Carl put his finger to his lips and pointed at Canon. After Canon took his shot and missed, Carl mentioned that Ms. Payne had arrived. Canon turned around and put down his pool cue and looked at Willow. He saw a gorgeous 6-foot black woman of thirty years. She was wearing a gold ski suit zipped up in the front that showed her full figure.

"You play, Ms. Payne?"

"I try, Mr. Canon," she said and walked around the table and picked up a pool cue. "Since I'm the guest, I guess I'll break." Off the break, the eight ball went in the far-right pocket, winning her the game. "Another?"

"Yes another. You can break again. Like you said, you are my guest." Canon set up the rack and moved it off the table. Willow set up and broke the balls. The eight ball went in the far-left corner this time, winning her the game again. Canon looked at her, walked over to the bar and poured himself a Johnny Walker red over ice. He took a long swig and said, "Once more and this time, I'll break."

Willow racked up the balls for Canon and moved off the table. Canon broke and the 6 and 5 ball went off the table into separate pockets. Canon set up for the 3 ball in the side pocket and made it, and was set up for the number 2 and 7 right behind each other in the corner pocket. He made both, but fell behind the 4, 8 and 1. Canon tried to bank the 4 off the side to get to the one ball that was near the side pocket, and missed. Willow took over and dropped the 1 ball than the 4 and 8, winning her the game. She laid her stick on the table, walked over to the bar, and poured herself a gin and tonic.

"You don't believe in giving a person much of a chance, do you, Miss Payne? Where there's an opening, you go straight for it, don't you?"

"In my line of work, Mr. Canon, it really doesn't pay to linger. You have a nice home here. How many square feet is it?"

"6300 feet, more or less. 15 bedrooms, 20 baths, bowling alley, swimming pool, and 2 saunas, plus a firing range. You know, the usual."

"Mr. Canon, do you want to tell me why I'm here? I hadn't finished the job I was hired to do."

"Well, Ms. Payne. I had heard so much about you that I wanted to meet you in person. Plus, your next hit left his main location, and we're waiting to get word of where he'll be next. Meanwhile, I thought you could stop off here and maybe I could offer you a permanent job with my organization. Especially after Mr. Yen."

"I don't know, Mr. Canon. I've always worked alone, and what I mean by that is, no bosses. Only contracts. It seems to work out better for me in the end."

"Well, you are going to be here with us a few days, think about it."

The door opened and a lady of about 5 foot 4 walked in and said, "Mr. Canon, lunch is served." She was dressed in a butler uniform—white shirt and black bowtie. Her hair was tied up in a bun at the back of her head.

"Are all the ladies there?" Canon asked.

"Just as you ordered, sir," she replied.

"Thank you, Ornette. Ms. Payne, its lunch time, come."

Willow noticed it was near 3 PM and said, "It's a little late for lunch, isn't it?"

"Lunch is when I say it is, Ms. Payne. Come."

CHAPTER 6

Willow Meets the Girls

The dining room was "large". The table was at least 25 feet long, with a large king size chair at the head and eight chairs on each side, and one smaller at the other end. Carl was sitting there with some of the most beautiful girls Willow had ever seen. The table was loaded with shrimp, lobster, Simons, swordfish, scallops, hush puppies, and salads of all kinds. There was also duck and pheasant under glass. The drinks that were served included tea, lemonade, champagne, and Mai Tais. She noticed one thing: a few of the girls didn't look too happy. She found out later that those would be replaced with the new batch of girls that were seated at the left of Canon. Canon's number one girl was named Sisley and she came to the table late. As soon as Willow saw her, she recognized her as their missing agent. She took the chair right next to Canon, he kissed her on the forehead and she smiled politely. Willow was sitting on the other end with Carl and he explained to her why so many of the girls were there.

"The girls on the left have been here for a year or more and Mr. Canon gets rid of at least two or three of them and replaces them. The ones on the right have only been here a few days and he may or may not keep them."

"What happens to the ones he let's go?"

"You don't want to know."

"The one sitting beside Mr. Canon—Sisley—how long has she been here?"

"She's fairly new. She has only been here two to three months. The boss likes her, so she may be around for a while."

"How do such beautiful girls get here?"

"White slavers, pirates, renegades, and all kinds of ways. We pick out the best ones for Mr. Canon but that's not our trade. We leave that for others."

"Which girl is yours, Carl?"

Carl just looked at her and said, "The help is not allowed to touch, until they're on their way out."

"Like now," Willow said.

After lunch, Canon took Willow for a stroll around his property. The only way up to it from the valley was by helicopter, and its location was secret. There was a trail but it was very steep and could only be passed by Jeep. Some have tried and ended up at the bottom of the mountain.

There was another trail behind the home, with trees that led up to a mountain with a 500 foot drop straight down. Canon had professionals try and scale it and they told him it could be done but only by professionals. He kept a guard there anyway. There was at least six other guards around the home, including two females, their dogs, and one bear that was always let out after dark.

"No one is allowed to go outside the house after dark."

"Has anyone ever tried to escape?"

"Yes, one." Willow never asked what happened to her. She expected it was probably nothing good.

Canon said. "The cooks come and go every other week by helicopter; otherwise, they stay in the back part of the house that's set up for them. Would you like to see the bear?"

"No, I don't think so. When you've seen one bear, you've seen them all. Carl said you were out skiing when I came in this morning."

"Yes, just over the bluff there," he said and pointed to a trail leading up from the house. "Snow's still heavy over that way. Do you ski?"

"Some," Willow replied.

"Yeah, I'll bet," Canon said. "about like you play pool," he said smiling.

Back at the house, near Willow's room door, Carl said, "I'll leave you here and meet you in the lounge at 9 PM. Kim will come around to fetch you. Looking forward to it."

The lounge was huge with a fireplace that spanned from floor to ceiling with an opening so wide, anyone could just about walk into. Above it, portraits of Canon hung of him sitting in an overstuffed chair and smoking a pipe. He was wearing a white shirt that opened at the collar, with a black smoking jacket and lounge pants. The lounge also had two eight-foot long brown leather couches with two matching chairs of the same color. It boasted a twenty-five-foot bar with mirrors behind it and bottles of liquor featured in front of it. The floor was carpeted and soundproof –

nothing was heard as one walked across the floor. The walls had paintings by Van Gogh and Rembrandt, while the other wall showcased a work by Picasso and Monet, separated by a vase in between.

Willow walked in wearing a chiffon dress cut above the knees with high heels of the same color, elevating her height to 6'1. She wore a jade necklace and earrings, with two diamond rings on one hand and three on the other. One ring stood out on her right hand; it had the head of Medusa on it, and the snakes' heads were made of jade. Canon's eyes lit up when he saw her, even though he had just seen her hours earlier.

CHAPTER 7

Assassin Reviled

He stood up and said, "Ms. Payne, come sit by me over here on the couch."

Sisley was also there, and Carl was sitting on one of the chairs. Canon had Sisley sit to his side and had Willow sit on the other. He put a hand on each one's knee and looked at both and shook his head, "Un UN UN, two fine ladies—it doesn't get any better than this."

Kim walked out the room and closed the door behind her.

"Carl, would you please pour the drinks?"

After serving the drinks, Carl sat back in his seat and crossed his legs.

"Ms. Payne, I don't think you've met Sisley, even though we all had lunch together. You never were introduced."

Willow nodded at Sisley, who then said, "Nice to meet you."

That's her, all right, Willow thought. She estimated her height to be around 5'4 or 5'5 – she couldn't tell that well at the luncheon. *Blond, mold under her lip.* If Willow couldn't see all that then, she could surely see now as this woman stood no more than three feet away.

"What type of work are you in, Ms. Payne – if I might ask?"

Willow looked at her then glanced at Canon. She replied that she was in the disposal business and trash removal.

Canon said, "Sisley, that's not a question you should be asking Ms. Payne."

"Oh, that's okay, Mr. Canon. We're among friends here, I hope. So, what work are you into?" Sisley asked again.

"I'm an assassin. I kill people."

Sisley's mouth dropped open. "Oh! Oh! You're joshing right?"

"No, I do not 'josh.'"

Sisley sat back on the couch and remained quiet. Canon looked at her and asked her if she had any more questions. She shook her head.

"Sisley, I'd like to talk to Ms. Payne alone. Do you mind?"

Sisley got up from the couch, said good night to Canon and Carl, before looking at Willow and leaving the room.

"Do you think you should have told her that, Ms. Payne?"

"I believe in honesty, Mr. Canon—even if I may have to kill her later."

"Ms. Payne, we have some news for you," Carl interjected. Steger has departed for the U.S.—Texas, to be exact. Somewhere around Austin city limits. We'll know exactly where soon."

"That was fast – you must have an excellent Intel system."

"I do, but I can't take all the credit."

"Carl has a lot to do with it. We should know in a day or two where he'll be and you can take him out from there."

"Any problems with you going to Texas?" Carl asked.

"Not one bit. When do I leave?"

3:45 AM. Sisley woke up in her room with a hand covering her mouth. Her eyes widened. Willow told her to be quiet and said the word "beacon," the password agent Stone had given her to say to Sisley when she located her. She informed her it will be at least another week before they could leave and to get ready. Before Willow left, Sisley asked her if she was really an assassin.

In Texas, near Austin city limits in the hill country, Willow got out of the Jeep she had rented and walked down the hill overlooking the cabin at the bottom. She was sporting her backpack and holding a rifle and scope, along with three clips knife on her right boot and the Japanese throwing knife tucked underneath her shirt behind her back. The camouflage clothing she wore made it almost impossible to see her in the woods. At the last minute, she had a change of heart and decided to ask agent Stone for the anti-aircraft missile, which she had used in Korea. On her last recon, she had noticed a propane tank beside the house that should work just fine for her mission.

The day before Willow, she had walked up the path. In the middle was an eight-foot diamond back rattlesnake, with its rattlers warning her not to come any closer.

"One of us is gonna have to move," she said. However, the snake stayed where it was and so did she. Willow eventually pulled out her Japanese throwing knife. She took it by the tip of the blade and in a flash, she threw it toward the snake and into its head. She watched as it thrashed around before walking over and removing the knife out of its head. She cut off its tail with its five rattlers, and put them in her back pocket. *Never know when you might need a good set of rattlers*, she thought.

CHAPTER 8

The Doodad

"Agent stone, have you heard from Willow? Did she find our agent?"

"Yes, sir, she even had a word with her. Canon has her on the mountain in his home. She's been there about 3 months but she can't call out. She is alive. Willow advised she had to go to Texas, in the Austin area to take out Steger then back to the mountainside. Canon had offered her a job, but she put him off. Once she gets back, she plans on killing Canon and his number one. There are also ten to fifteen girls she wants to release. I think the old girl is getting soft. The old Willow, the killer, wouldn't think about anything but getting the job done."

"We all change, agent Stone. It takes some longer than others."

"She has a request—you know that little doodad we sent her in Korea? Well, she found another use for it."

"Whatever she needs. Texas—has she ever been there before?"

"Only once, when she and Dorothy went to Houston trying to locate Jesse. I have a feeling the Texan heat is going to kill her, if Steger doesn't do it first. But there is no doubt she'll get the job done. Contact our people in Austin to be on alert, just in case she needs help."

"If she does, sir, that may blow our operation and our agent there will be entirely on her own."

"We can only wish her success."

Willow focused on the propane tank twenty yards from the house. What she needs is a 'twofer' – a two- for-one shot. Four men were in the cabin, with Steger being one of them. She thought of going for the sure shot, right through the front door. She laid a second missile round next to the first and loaded up. One of the men came out of the cabin and walked to one of the cars, opened its trunk and retrieved two rifles, which he carried inside.

"There is no time like the present," she said as she put the launcher up to her shoulder and fired. Once the rocket hit the cabin, she loaded the next round and fired at the propane tank. It exploded and the flames shot toward the cabin, causing a large fireball. Only one man came out of the cabin running and screaming as he was on fire. He headed toward one of the cars but the fire had reached it first and the vehicle blew up. The whole area was in flames and the one man was blown right back in. The cabin, cars, propane tank all went up in smoke.

Willow had begun putting away her equipment and was preparing to leave when she noticed two riders on horseback emerging from the woods on the other side of the cabin.

Willow raised her binoculars to see who the newcomers were. The one riding the pinto was wearing a black, wide brim cowboy hat with a silver band, as well as a leather vest with little bells hanging from its fringes. The other rider was wearing a black derby and had a handlebar mustache. He wore a red bandanna, plaid shirt and was riding a black stallion. While looking at them, one of the riders had stopped and was also looking at Willow through his own binoculars. He pointed to where Willow was and they headed quickly in her direction. She ran up the hill as fast as she could, with her backpack in hand. Her Jeep was half a mile away, and it was going to be a race to beat the horsemen. They, on the other hand, didn't head directly up the hill but to where her Jeep was parked. Willow ran and fell repeatedly but saw the Jeep that was within sight. Approximately 150 yards away from the Jeep, the riders broke out of the trees and into the clearing. They rode like a bat out of hell to get to Willow before she reached her car. She was running like she had never ran before, knowing she would be dead if she doesn't make it in time. Twenty-five yards short, Willow lost the race. The riders reached the Jeep and started slowly riding their mounts toward her. She stopped, sat down on her backpack and rested. The riders came up to her and looked at her.

"Well, I'll be goddamned, Roy. I'd never seen a lady hit a person before. She's damn right pretty. What you think we should do with her? After all, the boss is dead and there's no one to pay us now."

"Well, Jerome, I'll tell you where my mind is, and that is getting me some of this black pussy. Sound good to you?"

"Damn right Roy, and then we can kill her."

By that time, Willow had regained her composure and breath. She told them, "Listen, fellows. You know your boss is dead and you have no way of getting paid. I can help you there. I'll double whatever your boss was paying you – all you have to do is walk away. After all, I don't think Steger meant that much to you – he was just a paycheck."

"How about this, miss? We get the honey and the money too?"

Willow looked up at them and said, "You can't have both. Take the money."

"We'll take the honey and the money," they replied, as they started to dismount from their horses. Willow had her hand in her back pocket. She grabbed the rattlers and rattled them as loudly as she could. The horses became agitated and recoiled, throwing the men off their backs. After hitting the ground, Roy tried to reach for the gun on his side but Willow had thrown her throwing knife into his throat before he could do it.

When Jeremy fell, his horse fell on top of him and he lost his gun. The horse ran off and Willow ran over and retrieved it. *A forty-five—nice*, she thought as she looked at Jeremy, who was sitting on the ground and holding his leg. He looked at her and held up his hand. He said, "Is it too late to take the money?"

Willow shot him between the eyes. "Sorry. Yes, it's too late."

Breaking news...Austin Texas

In the hills above Austin, Texas, a cabin caught fire. It is believed to be propane-related. Four occupants were found dead. With the propane located too close to the cabin, two vehicles were also destroyed. Three miles away, two other men were also found dead. Two horses were found with saddles and grazing nearby, one of the two had a wound in his throat, while the other had a bullet hole between his eyes; the authorities are investigating.

Willow was sitting on the patio of a café and having lunch – tea and a shrimp salad. Her tan, cotton shorts were midway up her thigh She wore a see-through halter, revealing her nipples. She had her legs crossed underneath the table and still had on her necklace. The straw hat she wore had a wide brim that covered most of her back and half of her face, while her Foster Grant shades covered her nose and eyes. The 92 °F weather was almost tolerable but she was glad to leave Texas. Her cell phone rang.

"Ms. Payne, your car will be there in approximately 30 minutes to take you to the airport."

"Thank you so much."

Once at the airport, she departed for Europe.

Upon arrival, Canon had his helicopter waiting to bring her back to his place in the mountain.

CHAPTER 9

Your Turn!

Willow got out of the helicopter and was met by Carl, who brought her to Canon's home.

"Congratulations on your success in Texas. I'm sure Mr. Canon would like to see you, but he's on the ski slope right now."

Carl escorted her to her room and left. After taking a bath, she went down to the lounge, only to find Sisley in the billiard room.

"How was your trip?" Sisley asked.

"Oh, uneventful. How have you been coming along with Canon?"

"Good and bad news—he brought another girl here and I went from being his number one to his number two."

"Well, that's okay. It's time to get you out of here anyway. But first, we'll deal with Mr. Canon."

"They'll be sending the girls out of here in a few days, so we have to move before then. He goes skiing but he only takes his bodyguards with him."

"So, you're saying the slope is the only place to get close to him?"

"Well, there is the helicopter that he uses about once or twice a month to go into the village, but then you'll have to kill the pilot and you wouldn't want to do that."

"You ever hear of collateral damage?"

At that moment, one of the girls burst into the room and said, "Mr. Canon just came in. He is being helped by his guards. It look like he has broken his leg." Willow and Sisley looked at each other and there was a hint of a smile on Willow's lips. Well, I guess we should go see if we can be of any assistance. Canon was laying on the couch in the lounge with a splint on his leg. He was moaning and cursing. Carl was on the phone talking to the local doctor.

"Yeah, he was on the slope when it happened. I will send the helicopter for you. Carl, bring me a drink, a large one. It looks like this bone is trying to come out of the skin." Willow and Sisley walked into the room, followed by the messenger girl. Canon looked at them and they could see right away that he was in pain.

"Is there anything we can do?" she asked.

"Before this happened, there was a lot you could have done." He downed his drink. "Now, you can get me another drink." Willow didn't move but looked at the girl that came in with them.

"Why is he in here?" Willow asked. "He should be in his bedroom!"

"Yeah, that's right," Canon said. "It takes an outsider to run things around here. Carl, why didn't you think of that? How long before the doctor gets here?"

"A little over an hour, give or take."

"Give or take, my ass. It better be less than an hour. Where is my goddamn drink? You making that shit over there? Put it in a water glass. I know that the doctor is going to be probing the hell out of me, may as well be fucked up when he gets here."

The guards took Canon to his room. Carl and the message girl followed and Willow and Sisley stayed in the room. They walked over to the bar and poured themselves a drink.

"The plans seem to be changing. I think now is a good time to contact agent Stone."

Almost two hours later, the doctor arrived. He was a short heavy-set man with hair only on the side of his head and back. The top of his head was completely bald. He wore wire rim spectacles, a smock, and hospital attire, and carried a black doctor's bag.

"Sorry for the delay, but you caught me in the middle of an operation," he said in a high-pitched voice.

"You're here now doc, get to work."

By the time he reached Canon, he was out cold from consuming a fifth and a half of scotch.

"This is better than I could have expected. Most of my patients are up and raising plenty of hell by this time." He examined Canon's leg.

"This is a bad break. We need to get him down to the clinic right away, I can do more for him there."

"I don't know, doc. Mr. Canon hardly ever leaves these mountains except for business or emergencies."

"What do you think this is, young man? And who's in charge now that Mr. Canon is incapacitated?"

"I am, my name is Carl."

"Well, Carl. You need to make a decision, either we take him to the clinic or try to work on him here; in which case, we may end up having to amputate his leg. Is that what you want?"

"You don't understand, doc. Mr. Canon has enemies, and it wouldn't be good for him to be caught in town without any kind of security."

"What do those men do, there in front of the house? They can't go with him?"

"I guess they could, but there's no need for all of them being here."

"Adolf, Ralf, take Mr. Canon to the helicopter, and you'll be going to the village with him. Take Homer and Otto with you. I'll be down in a day or two. That's gonna leave only three guards here to guard the girls and six will be leaving tomorrow. Two will have to go with them to the port, leaving me to watch the other five alone."

After Canon and the guards left, Carl was in the lounge having a drink, when Ms. Payne came in, walked over to the bar, and poured herself a gin and tonic.

"What's up, Carl? You don't look so good."

"You're right about that, Ms. Payne. I've never been in this situation before. After tomorrow, I'll be down to one person, and that's me."

Carl went on to tell her his predicament. Then, she said, "How can I help?"

"I'm glad you ask, Ms. Payne. I was just thinking about that. I may need you to watch the girls while I go to the village and check on Mr. Canon. The other men will take the girls to the port. It should take no more than twenty-four hours."

CHAPTER 10

The Take Down

71

"Agent Stone, this is Janice."

"We were worried about you, Janice. How's it going?"

"It's about to move around here, and I think we'll be wrapping it up soon. Canon broke his leg in a ski accident; he's in the village at the clinic. They're moving six of the girls out tomorrow by helicopter to the port. You can grab them there. They're not sending Sisley. She'll be here with me and the five other girls. The only person who will be here after the girls leave is Carl, and we'll handle him."

"What will you need from us, other than grabbing the girls at the port?"

"Just some transportation. The only way to get here is by helicopter, so I'll give you the coordinates."

"One thing, Janice. What about Canon? We have nothing to pick him up on and he'll still be out there. Right now, Canon has four guards around him but if there was a way to distract them..."

"I understand, Janice—leave it to us."

The next day after the girls had gone, the only ones left in the house with Carl was Sisley, Willow and five girls. Carl entered Sisley's room.

"It's that time, babe and I've been wanting you ever since you got here. Now is the time."

"Canon won't like what you're doing, Carl. So you better back off."

"You're forgetting, Sisley—you're no longer number one and I get all leftovers."

He moved towards Sisley and ripped off the thin nightgown she had on, leaving her with nothing but panties and bra. He looked at her and started undressing. Sisley made a dash for the door, but Carl beat her to it and locked it shut.

"Now, look, Sisley. You're not being realistic. I'm going to get what I want and there is no way around it. There is no place for you to go, and you'll never leave here, believe me. So, give it up. Plus, Canon gave you to me. You should've known that by his having moved you to being his number two."

"Forget it, Carl. I'm not going to do it."

"That's bullshit. I've been wanting you too long. I want it and I want it now." Carl ran towards Sisley, tackled her and threw her on the bed. He started ripping off her bra and panties. She fought as best she could, then said, "Okay, okay—Carl, you win. Let's get this over with."

She stopped fighting him. "Let me get these torn panties off. Lay back on the bed."

"No bullshit now, Sisley," said Carl. "I don't want to have to hurt you."

After the panties were off, she laid down on the bed beside Carl. She started kissing his neck and chest, his ear lobe and his face. When she felt him getting an erection, she took his face in her hands and kissed him on the lips, slipped her tongue into his mouth. She bit his lips lightly at first, then put a little pressure on it. Carl had a tight grip on her arms and around her waist, later moving his hands to grab her butt. Seconds into the kiss, the pressure he had on her decreased and went slack; another few seconds, he removed all pressure completely. Sisley looked at Carl. His eyes and mouth were wide open, and he wasn't moving. She jumped out of bed and looked at him again. She took his pulse. He was dead, just like Willow said he would be.

11:45 AM Three helicopters converged on Mountainside Lodge. One had agents Stone and Jenkins onboard, another had 12 commandos and the last was empty to transport the girls and staff. Janice and Sisley met them at the heliport.

"Damn Janice, did you leave anything for us? Who's here?"

"Just the girls and the help, cooks and cleaning people. They'll go back with the girls. Sisley and I searched the Lodge as best we could. We found some papers but I think most of what we need will be in the safes we had found—oh yes! In one of the bedrooms, you'll find a dead body: Canon's right hand, Carl."

"Have you located Canon? Is he still at the clinic?"

"Sure is," Janice replied.

"With two men outside his room and two at the local hotel?"

"We can remove those two on some charge or another. As for the other two, we have no idea what to do with them. Maybe after we check the contents of the safes, we'll have something on them but not right now. We saw Canon has a cast on his leg, from the knee to his toe."

"How about this? Why don't we let Canon and his two men return to the Lodge, and I'll deal with them there? Otherwise, we'll be dealing with them for years to come in court."

"The pilot seems to be okay but I'll let you determine that."

"Do you want Sisley to stay with you? Or anyone else?"

"No, she's been here long enough. She can tell you quite a bit about Canon's operation."

"Then you can handle the three who are returning?"

"Well, 2 and 1/2 really—and yes, I can handle them."

Upon boarding the helicopter, Sisley asked Willow about the drug she gave Carl.

"It's something I had used on another case and I had found it to be useful. It takes a target out without a fuss. It's fast-acting poison that's in a fake tooth. Once you bite down on his tongue, it releases poison. The risk is if you happen to bite your own tongue. Then, you're out of here. I hope you discarded the cap."

"How did you know that Carl would come after me when everyone left?"

"He just about told me so, and this was the perfect opportunity for him. Now, you better go."

At 8 PM that night, Canon and his two guards arrived at the lodge. Stepping out of the helicopter, he noticed there were no guards around nor were any dogs barking. He looked over toward the cage where the bear was housed. No bear in sight.

"Where the hell is everyone?" he said out loud. "Homer, check the perimeter for the men."

As Homer came around the corner of the lodge, he ran into Willow.

"Ms. Payne, where is everyone?"

"Homer, it's better if I show you rather than tell you." Then, she shot him between the eyes. In the lounge, Canon was draped on the couch and he asked Adolph to bring him a drink.

"Go see if you can find Carl. And send Sisley to me." Adolph walked over to the lodge, billiard room, hot tub, the girls area and Carl's room. There was no one. On the way back, he ran into Willow.

"Ms. Payne, where is everyone?"

Willow lifted the 22 automatic with its silencer and shot Adolph right between the eyes. He dropped right where he stood.

Willow walked into the lounge. When Canon saw her, he asked, "Ms. Payne, where the hell is everyone?"

"First of all, Mr. Canon, my name is not 'Ms. Payne.' Second, everyone is gone—the girls, cooks, Carl, Sisley and your men—they're all gone."

"Gone where? What the hell are you talking about?"

"The authorities have them. Your entire operation has gone, by the way of Mr. Yen and Steger. You're the only one left and pretty soon, you'll be gone, too."

"So, you lied? Everything you said was a lie? What haven't you told me that wasn't a lie?"

"When I told you I was an assassin—that wasn't a lie." Then, he noticed the automatic she brought out from behind her back.

"Time to pay the piper, Mr. Canon."

She then shot him once between the eyes before walking up to him and shooting him twice more in the head. She walked over to the bar and put her weapon down. She poured herself a gin and tonic and sat down in one of the plush chairs. The door opened and in walked the pilot holding a 45 automatic.

"I noticed Adolph's body in the hallway and Homer's outside the lodge. I put two and two together and I came up with—I sure didn't want to believe that you were a hit woman. I didn't believe him. That'll teach me."

"Now that you have all this information, what are you going to do with it?"

"I could just blow your ass away—right here, right now."

"Then, why don't you? You seem to have all the power. Of course, you no longer have an employer but you do still

81

have that helicopter. You can find employment elsewhere."

The pilot thought about it for a minute. "You know, you may be right—except Mr. Canon has been good to me for many years! Fuck it. I'll be leaving now."

He headed towards the door and closed it behind him. Janice took another drink and stood up. She picked up her 22 automatic and with both hands, she a pointed it at the door and waited. Seconds later, the pilot threw open the door, gun in hand and yelled, "I changed my mind!" Willow shot him three times in the chest.

Epilogue

A week later, Willow walked in the apartment she shared with Keisha, threw her bags on the living room floor and said, "Honey, I'm home!"

After looking around, she headed to the bedroom and found Keisha sitting on the bed, crying. Willow ran over to her, took her face in her hands and saw the black eye.

"What happened? Stop crying and tell me what happened."

"Janice, don't get involved. It's too much for you to handle. A couple of girls have already been beaten up."

"Would you just tell me what happennd?"

"Extortion! Some men are trying to extort money from us stewardesses."

"How long has this been going on?"

"Since right after you left. I didn't want to call and upset you, but we just can't handle it."

"What about the police? Have they been notified of this?"

"No, they warned us about going to the police. One of the girls had tried—she was the one that got beat up."

"How many men are we talking about?"

"At least three. And they are mean, Janice—I mean, real mean."

"Go to the bathroom and take a shower. Get yourself cleaned up and we'll talk once you're out."

"Janice, you think you'll be able to help us?"

"We'll see, baby. We'll see."

Keisha had no idea what line of work Janice did, only that she knew people and that her work took her away from home for weeks at a time. She never knew that having Janice Willow for a friend was like having her own personal assassin, and that she had just signed the death certificate of those three men.

Other books by this author:

Enlisted at 14…A Memoir

Enlisted at 14 and the journey continues

Enlisted at 14… Looking back

Willow… A novel

Willow… One for the team

Willow… And the Medusa

Little Miss Willow… A Short Story

Meet Ruben Kane

R.K. {Ruben Kane}

Assassin

Ruben's bag

Ruben's bad side

Smooth…A Ruben Kane novel

Ducks in a row

Just a dream

Dream Catcher

Next in the willow series:

""Blacker the Berry"

www.ingramcontent.com/pod-product-compliance
Lightning Source LLC
Chambersburg PA
CBHW070534130626
46555CB00003B/1405